love among t…

BOOK FOUR

The Land Across the Sea

M. KATHERINE CLARK

Copyright © 2020 by M. Katherine Clark

Cover Design by M. Katherine Clark

All rights reserved. No part of this book may be reproduced or transmitted in any form or by any means, electronic or mechanical, including but not limited to photocopying, recording, or by any information storage and retrieval system, without permission in writing from the Author or representatives.

This is a work of fiction. Names, characters, places, and incidents are the product of the author's imagination or are used fictitiously, and any resemblance to any actual persons, living or dead, events, or locals is entirely coincidental.

All rights reserved.

ISBN-13: 978-0-9998708-8-4

Other works by M. Katherine Clark

The Greene and Shields Files
- Blood is Thicker Than Water
- Once Upon a Midnight Dreary
- Old Sins Cast Long Shadows
- Tales from the Heart, Novelettes

Love Among the Shamrocks Collection
- Under the Irish Sky
- Across the Irish Sea
- On the River Shannon
- The Land Across the Sea, an Emmet O'Quinn Short

Love Among the Shamrocks Collection the Next Generation
- In Dublin Fair City
- Song of Heart's Desire
- Chasing After Moonbeams – Coming 2021

The Wolf's Bane Saga
- Wolf's Bane
- Lonely Moon
- Midnight Sky
- Star Crossed
- Moon Rise
- Moon Song, a Companion Guide

Dragon Fire
- Heart of Fire
- Will of Fire – Coming 2021

Soundless Silence, *a Sherlock Holmes Novel*
The Rest is Silence, *an Edmond Holmes Novel* – Coming 2021
Silent Whispers, *a Scottish Ghost Story*
Silent Night, *a Scottish Christmas Ghost Story* – Coming Soon

For the Emmet O'Quinn fans! He went through a lot in Across the Irish Sea. This takes place between On the River Shannon and during the four years in his book.

Enjoy!

Trevor ran into his grandfather's arms as soon as they were past airport security. Curtis scooped him up and kissed his cheek. Emmet walked up slowly, hearing Trevor tell his grandparents about the flight and how they stopped off in Philadelphia for a day and went to the zoo. His son loved the zoo and animals. It wouldn't surprise him if he became a veterinarian like Emmet's brother Cabhan. The thought of animals invariably brought back the memory of Jacks, Emmet's beloved black lab. Jacks had gotten sick and died three months ago and the pain was horribly fresh. Emmet wondered if everything that happened was God's way of punishing him. He was damned if he knew for what. But then again, he didn't believe in God anyway, so that could be why.

Curtis looked over at him and nodded. Joann hurried to Emmet and embraced him. Startled at first, he eventually hugged back. He knew they had developed a sort of understanding and, dare he say, friendship but her welcome made him smile.

"Welcome to Indiana," Joann gushed.

"Thank you," Emmet replied. "I need to pick up my bags."

"This way," Curtis said, and they followed him through the Indianapolis International Airport. Emmet forced himself not to react when Joann slipped her hand through his arm.

"Now, we've made up the room next to Trevor's. It was Jennifer's old room," she looked away for a moment and Emmet didn't miss how she wiped her tears and cleared her throat. "I know that might be a little bit strange, but it's a nice room. I understand you want your own space but you are welcome to stay as long as you like and save money while doing it. But if you have hotel reservations, we understand."

Emmet didn't answer right away. He wanted, no, needed his space after everything but it would help to have someone there besides Trevor to help him not slip deeper into a depression. Saving money was important too. After picking up his entire life and moving to America in six short months, not to mention the price of a visa, shipping costs, and plane tickets, he needed to replenish his savings.

"Thank you, Joann. So long as it's not too much trouble for you, I would like to stay for a time at least."

"Not too much trouble at all. I'd love it!" Joann said. "I know you'll want your own space, and we'd be happy to show you around some nice apartment complexes. But until you get settled, stay with us."

"I appreciate that, thank you."

"Or are you looking at buying? The market is good right now."

"No, not yet," Emmet admitted. "I want to get settled and on my feet first."

"Understandable. Well, let's get your bag and head out. If you aren't too tired. We were hoping to take you and Trevor along with our other daughter's family to dinner tonight. You didn't get to meet Charlotte, did you?"

"Only in passing," he replied.

"Well, she asked to meet you properly. Her husband, Derek is home from a business trip and is hoping to meet you. But if it's too much, we can reschedule."

Emmet thought for a long moment. As tired as he was, he barely slept on the plane, he knew he needed to make nice with Trevor's family if he had any hope of surviving.

"That'd be nice, thank you. I insist on paying."

"Nonsense," Curtis tossed over his shoulder. "It would be my pleasure."

Emmet wanted to argue but he bit his tongue. One thing he learned, Curtis was a proud man and did not take a challenge well.

Finding his checked luggage, he followed his son's grandparents out of the airport and into the warm summer day. Emmet swallowed thickly. The humidity was about the same as home but as the sun beat down on them, Emmet immediately broke out in a sweat. It was nearly thirty degrees warmer in Indiana than Killarney.

Emmet enjoyed hot, sunny weather as much as the next person, but he preferred to have a margarita in hand and lounge on the beach with his feet in the sand, than to be wearing jeans and a dress shirt.

Curtis led them to a white SUV and unlocked the doors. As Curtis buckled Trevor in the backseat, Emmet secured his suitcase and duffle in the trunk. Having sent most of his things earlier, he only had the essentials packed. Things like his hurling sticks, kitchen wears, and pictures were in storage just down the road from Curtis and Joann. He sent most of his clothes to their house last week; not that he could fit in any of them anymore, he scoffed.

Emmet opened the door for Joann and was rewarded by a pat on the cheek and a smiled "such a gentleman" as she got in.

The drive from the airport to Curtis' and Joann's suburban neighborhood gave Emmet a chance to see Indiana. Well, the highway mostly, but he did admit it was lovely. The conversation steered mostly to his cousin Keera's wedding and how his sister-in-law Ness was doing as a new mother. It reminded him to text his family to let them know he had landed and would call later.

The jet lag was getting to him as he stared at the late afternoon hour on the dash, he yawned. Trevor had fallen asleep in his booster seat and Emmet realized with a start, he would need to get a car, learn how to drive backwards, and know how to safely navigate the roads before he got a booster seat for his son. Owning a car dealership in Killarney, he knew how to drive either left or righthand side

The realization of what he had done and all he had yet to do, came crashing down on him. He felt a panic attack coming as the sides of the car closed in. His breathing picked up, but he suppressed as much of it as he could not wanting to look weak in their eyes. His father was right, he was strong but sometimes strength needed help. Maybe he should have seen a psychologist, but he thought he could handle it. All the changes that happened in his life in the last ten months, had his head spinning.

"Are you all right, Emmet?" he heard Curtis ask and looking up, he caught Curtis' eye in the rearview mirror. Emmet wiped his sweaty palms on his jeans, took a deep breath and nodded.

"Sorry, thanks. Do you mind if I lower my window?"

"Of course," Curtis replied, and Emmet gulped in the hot but fresh air.

"We know what a large sacrifice you have made for us, and we are sorry it was under those circumstances but happy to have you here," Joann said. "I know it's not exactly where you imagined you would be right now."

"Not at all, actually," he spat, then sighed. "I'm sorry. You don't deserve my anger, at all."

"We do but thank you. We did not make it easy for you. And we are very sorry for it," Joann replied. Emmet waved it off.

"If I heard some stranger was going to take my grandson away, I would not have been as nice as you were," Emmet said.

"But you weren't some stranger. You are Trevor's father and I feel like I know you from all the stories Jenny… Jenny told," Joann's voice cracked when she said her daughter's name. Forcing out a breath, she plastered a smile. "But we do understand. If there's anything we can do to help you settle in and adjust, please don't hesitate to ask."

"You've already done so much," Emmet answered.

"It was our pleasure."

He said nothing for a little while. "I don't suppose you can help me get used to driving on the wrong side of the street?"

Curtis and Joann chuckled. "I think I can. I taught both our daughters. I have more patience," Curtis winked.

"Yeah, right," Joann scoffed. "But yes, we'd be happy to

help. And when you are ready for your own place, I can help with shopping. I'm a bargain deal finder."

"That sounds great. I don't want our place to look like a bachelor pad. Trevor needs stability. Your help and maybe your daughter Charlotte's would be invaluable."

"We'd love to."

"I'd also like to get your help on finding a few pictures of Jennifer to have up. That way Trevor never forgets his mother."

He saw the tell-tale shimmer in Joann's eyes and her throat work as she looked away from the mirror.

"Of course," she said.

"Thank you."

"Here we are." Even Curtis' voice was tight. He pulled up to an elegant two story all brick home. It was impressive in a subdued way.

"You have a lovely home," he said.

"Thank you," Joann beamed.

Curtis parked in the driveway and turned the car off.

"I'll take him up and put him down for a nap. Can you get your bags?"

"Absolutely," Emmet replied.

"Come now. I'll show you in," Joann said as Curtis took Trevor into the house.

Joann took him through the garage, gesturing to the kitchen, which had a back stair up to the bedrooms. She showed the family room, dining room, and study. Then, she showed him into another room and he stopped.

"Beautiful," he breathed.

"The piano?" Joann questioned.

"Aye, a grand?"

"Extended baby grand," Joann corrected. "It was my grandfather's, he was a concert pianist and taught both my girls. It's been so long since I've heard music in the house. Both Jenny and Char play but since Jenny... Char hasn't wanted to play. I miss it."

"Would you... would you mind if I played occasionally?"

"You play?"

"I do. I had to learn when I first started working at the Plaza Hotel. The pianist in the restaurant bar was not reliable so I stepped in a few times. I fell in love with it. It was the only time I could truly express who I was."

"Of course. I would love it if you played! Any time. You never have to ask. And the doors close if you want some privacy but I would love to hear you."

"I'd be happy to play for you," he yawned. "Thank you."

"You poor thing, you must be exhausted. I can imagine."

"The stop off in Pennsylvania helped," Emmet admitted. "But it's been hard to sleep for a few... weeks."

"You mean months," she provided. "I understand. Have you talked to her?"

His eyes widened and he took a sharp breath in as if it was physically painful to him.

"No," he finally said. "And I appreciate your concern, but please let it be the end of it. I... it's too raw."

"Say no more, I'll not mention it again. I'm sorry."

"No, no it's fine. That is behind me, and all this is just waiting for me to explore. I am excited."

Whether Joann knew he was faking his enthusiasm, he wasn't sure, but she said nothing more about that, smiled slightly, and patted his arm. "Let me show you upstairs to your room. Get you comfortable."

"Thank you."

She led the way up the grand stairwell toward a room. Curtis slowly closed the door to another next door.

"He's out," Curtis whispered motioning to the door.

"He's tired," Emmet explained.

"Let's let you get settled. Can I bring you anything? A glass of wine, tea or a beer?" Joann offered.

"I've got a new bottle of whiskey," Curtis suggested. "I don't know if it's any good, but the man at the store said it was."

"I appreciate it, Curtis, but a wine would be nice for now, thank you. Maybe we can share a dram later?"

"Over a game. Do you play chess?" Curtis asked.

"I do, actually," Emmet replied.

"Excellent, I've been wanting to play with someone but my ladies don't play or want to learn. Maybe we can crack open the bottle over a game."

"I'd like that. I used to play every week with my da'."

"Well, I am no stand in for Orin, but I'd be happy to continue the tradition with you," Curtis said.

"Sure, of course."

"I'll get you that wine, you go ahead and get settled," Joann spoke next.

"I don't want you to wait on me, Joann. You have done enough more than enough." Emmet stopped her.

"It's what I love to do, Emmet. It's no bother at all."

"Very well."

"The closet has some space and the chest of drawers is cleaned out. I just couldn't bring myself to clear out all of her things." Curtis wrapped his arm around Joann's shoulders as tears gathered in her eyes.

"That's fine. I don't need much room," he replied.

"You can take however much room you need. I'll get you that glass of wine."

"Cheers, thanks," he said and watched them leave. Heaving a sigh, he stepped into the room and sat on the bed. "What the hell have I done?" he mumbled.

Visiting was one thing, but moving there? Then the thought of living in Ireland with all the memories of Mara and he shook his head. There was no way. This was his life and he needed to make the best of it.

He pulled out his phone and dialed his parent's. His dad answered almost immediately.

"Em?"

Damn, it was good to hear his voice. It had only been three days. How the hell was he supposed to make it through this? He saw his parents nearly every week and now, he wouldn't see them again for a very long time.

"Are you all right, lad?" his dad asked.

His chest constricted and he cleared his throat.

"Em?"

"Da', what the hell did I do? How am I going to survive this?"

"Hey, it's all right. It'll all be all right. You're being challenged. You're going through an ordeal, but you will come through it stronger and in one piece. You'll see. It may not feel that way now, but trust me, lad. I've been there. I *know* what you're going through. But I was not able to get away from it. You are. You have to grasp this new opportunity. You deserve it. You need to learn to live again."

"I'm sorry, da'," Emmet's voice wobbled.

"Sorry for what?" he questioned.

"For the hell I put you through when I was a boy. I didn't make your life easy after mum died and then when you met ma, I – I didn't understand. Now I do, you were able to talk to her. She was there for you to help you get over everything. I wish I knew then. I would never have done what I did."

"Hey no, enough of that," he stopped him. "Yes, Dierdre was there for me, still is. There are still times I miss Aislín so much and Dierdre isn't jealous nor is she hurt. She simply helps me. I am damn lucky to have found her, but I wasn't going to tell you that when you were a boy, you wouldn't have understood and I didn't want you to look at me as a lesser man. Now you don't just like I don't. I love you, son and I'm so damn proud of you and how you were able to move on and do the right thing for your son. That is what you must concentrate on and if you find a Dierdre, you hold on to her, understand?"

"Yes, sir."

"Good, lad. I love you, Emmet. Dee is asleep now, but I'll tell her you called but be sure to call again. She needs to hear from you."

"I'll call tomorrow."

"Talk to you soon," Orin promised.

"Love you, dad."

"Love you too, son."

Emmet hung up and unzipped his suitcase just as Joann knocked on the door with his wine.

Emmet enjoyed the glass of wine as he unpacked his suitcase. After twenty minutes, his eyes grew heavy and his body was weary. He did a quick calculation. If it was five o'clock it was ten over in Ireland. Usually one to stay up fairly late, Emmet blamed it on the medicine he still had to take for the occasional twinge of pain and a bunch of other things his brother assured him could happen even months after a bullet wound. Blood clots and death did not sound particularly interesting to him so he sucked it up and took his pills but they made him tired. He stared at the soft pillows and decided he had enough time for a quick nap, shower, and change for the dinner Curtis and Joann had planned. Pulling off his shirt and jeans, he kept his undershirt on. In all his thirty-six years, he had never been embarrassed of his body. Since he was young, he always maintained a movie star physique, but after he was shot and his doctor forbade anything strenuous, he lost what he had worked so hard to maintain. He knew it was vanity, but it was a comfort.

He was amazed at how easy it was to gain weight. Until he became comfortable in his new life and body, he would be keeping his shirts on.

The pillow was just as soft as he had thought it would be. Setting his alarm for one hour, he closed his eyes.

When next he opened his eyes, bright morning sunlight streamed through the windows in front of him. Blinking away sleep and his confusion, he reached for his phone to check the time. It was seven-thirty in the morning. Confused, Emmet checked his alarm. It was inactive. Sitting up, he pulled the sheets off him and wiped a hand down his face. Though he felt refreshed, guilt also poured over him.

Pulling on some sweat pants, he opened the door, immediately hearing Curtis' and Joann's voices down the stairs. The door next to his, where Trevor slept, was still closed. Easing it open, Emmet saw his son asleep, his little mouth open in the cutest way. He smiled and stared at the little miracle for a long moment. Many times over the last six months he had watched his son sleep. There was nothing more relaxing and fascinating to him in all the world. Trevor was the one good thing in his life. The main reason he fought to live.

Closing the door soundlessly, he trotted down the steps and followed the voices to the kitchen. As soon as he entered the area, Curtis looked up.

"Hey, there he is," he smiled.

Emmet looked around the room. A woman he had only seen briefly at the courthouse sat beside her father at the barstools. A man was with Joann in the kitchen, wearing a frilly apron, manning the griddle.

"Good morning, sorry. I set my alarm to get up in an hour. Not sure what happened," Emmet explained.

"It went off, honey," Joann replied, and he tried not to react to the term of endearment. "When you didn't turn it off after a little while, I knocked then snuck in to make sure you were okay. You were sound asleep. I turned it off for you. You needed your sleep. Don't worry, Trevor is still asleep from yesterday's nap too."

"Sorry I ruined the plans for last night," Emmet said.

"Nothing ruined. We'll go tonight. Not to worry. Besides Derek and Charlotte came over this morning," Curtis said indicating the two people he did not know.

"Hey yeah, good to meet you," Emmet offered his hand to Derek, who had to wipe it on his apron then Charlotte.

"Sorry, batter," Derek replied showing the pan of odd shaped pancakes. "And no, this isn't my apron." He teased.

"I told you Curtis' apron is in the wash," Joann said with a teasing lilt.

"Besides, babe," Charlotte began. "You look cute in frills."

"Yes, dear," the blonde-haired man turned and winked at his wife.

"Sorry we didn't get a chance to meet properly, Emmet," Charlotte turned to him. "But I feel like I know at least a little about you from Jen."

"Aye, sorry we didn't get a chance to meet either. I wanted to, but, ehm… things happened."

"Yeah, glad you're okay. How are you feeling?" Charlotte

asked.

"I'm good, cheers," Emmet stated. "But tired. I have to take a medicine to prevent blood clots for another two months before I'm *out of the woods*. The flight wore me out."

"Flights are brutal, man. Especially time zone changes," Derek said as he flipped a pancake.

"You travel a lot?" Emmet asked.

"Nearly every other week," Derek replied. "But it's nice to be home."

"Would you like a coffee, Emmet? Or maybe juice? We have the makings of a mimosa," Joann asked.

"Coffee would be great."

"Anything in it?"

"Nah, especially not how I feel currently," he said on a yawn.

"Come sit," Charlotte beckoned to the stool next to her.

"Anything I can help with?" Emmet looked around the kitchen.

"We got it, honey, go sit with Char," Joann stated, handing him a mug of coffee. Emmet could smell the bitterness and couldn't wait to try it. Coffee was something he enjoyed almost as much as whiskey.

Sitting beside Charlotte, he took a sip and smiled. It was good.

"Mom loves that you're here," Charlotte leaned in and whispered. "She's been complaining that she doesn't have anyone stay over that she can take care of. She loves to host."

"I'm grateful," Emmet replied. "But I don't want to put her out."

"You aren't," Joann refilled her husband's coffee mug and smiled sweetly at him.

"So since I didn't get a chance to meet you properly and we didn't go out last night, we decided to come over this morning," Charlotte explained back to a usual tone. "Derek is the chef of the family. His pancake batter is amazing."

"Oh? Are you a professional chef?" Emmet asked her husband.

"No, I'm a retail buyer. Cooking is a hobby," Derek explained as he poured pancake batter over some cooked bacon strips.

Emmet's brows furrowed and Charlotte laughed. "Our son, Peter. He's five and unlike most five-year olds, he doesn't like chocolate chip pancakes, but he *loves* bacon covered in pancake."

"He might be on to something," Emmet admitted, then looked around for the little boy, not seeing him.

"I have plenty. I'll make a few more, if you'd like to try it," Derek offered.

"That'd be great."

The door to the powder room opened and a little blonde-haired boy walked in to the kitchen. Emmet assumed he was Peter.

"Is Trevor up yet?" he asked.

"Not yet, honey. He had a long day. I'm sure he'll be up soon," Charlotte said. "Come say hello to your Uncle Emmet."

Emmet nearly choked on the coffee he was sipping.

"Oh, sorry," Charlotte grimaced. "I should have asked if that was okay. Would you prefer Mr. O'Quinn? We talked about it earlier and to give Peter some semblance of who you are…"

"No, no, that's fine," Emmet waved her off. "Sorry, it took me off guard. I wasn't expecting to be accepted so quickly."

"I know, honey," Joann looked at her husband crossly. "And that's our fault."

"No one's fault," he assured. "Just different."

"Well," Charlotte picked up her son and sat him on her lap. "This is Peter. Peter, say hello to your Uncle Emmet."

"Hi, Uncle Emmet," Peter's small voice said.

"Hiya, lad, it's good to meet you."

He looked up at his mother. "He talks funny."

"You know why he talks funny?" Charlotte asked. Peter shook his head. "Then ask, respectfully."

"Why do you talk funny, Uncle Emmet?" Peter asked looking back at him.

"Well, I was born in a country called Ireland. Do you know where that is?" He asked.

Peter nodded emphatically. "Aunt Jenny showed me when she got back. She said it was really beautiful and she met an amazing person. She said he was Trevor's dad."

Emmet felt his chest constrict with guilt. He hadn't given the cute blonde a second thought after she left. It was a good time, a great time and he missed her when she left for about three days then he was on to the next woman. Jennifer told her little nephew about him, had carried his son for nine months, had raised him for two years, had written Emmet a letter telling him all about it, had told their son stories about him every night and he couldn't be bothered to even think of her once in those three years after she left. *What kind of man am I?* he questioned.

"I'm glad your aunt shared it with you, Peter. Maybe one of these years we all can go back so you can see it for yourself," Emmet's voice was tight and by the look mother and daughter shared, they heard it. "Peter, I want to talk to you a bit more, but I have to run to the restroom, all right?" He would have rushed to the toilet to throw up if he didn't think it might cause the five-year-old confusion. They wanted him to be part of the family but how could he? After everything? He didn't deserve their kindness. Not after he never thought about their daughter, sister, or aunt.

Peter nodded and Emmet nearly jumped up and ran to the bathroom. The dry heaves that happened hurt his chest, but he couldn't stop.

He barely heard the door open and only turned when he heard someone turn on the faucet. Joann placed a damp cloth on his neck. He shuddered from the chill, but it felt good.

"What happened, sweetie?" she asked. "Was it the *uncle* thing? You don't have to have him call you that, if you don't want."

Emmet shook his head. "It wasn't that."

"Then what, honey?" Joann asked.

"Why?"

"Why what?"

"I do not deserve any of this. None of it. I didn't think of

Jennifer again after our time together, but she did. She carried my son. She told her nephew. She told Trevor stories about me so he would know about me. She was constantly reminded of me when I was off doing god only knows, not giving her a second thought. And now, you've taken me into your home and hearts... I don't deserve it. Any of it."

Joann knelt on the floor with him and pulled him into her when tears threatened. He tried to hold them off. He was a thirty-four-year-old man, he kept telling himself. *Get over it.* He thought. But he couldn't and the tears fell.

"This right here is exactly why you do deserve it, Emmet. What happened between you and Jennifer happened because you *both* wanted it. What happened after happened because *she* wanted it. She wanted to tell you. She wanted to talk to you so badly and it was Curtis and I who told her not to. We were cruel to you without even knowing you. But nothing we said dissuaded her from telling your son about you. So, you never thought about a vacation fling ever again, so what. It was your choice. Just as it was her choice to tell Trevor. Never once did she think about not telling him about you."

"Why did she keep him? Everything she went through alone. Why did she keep the child of a stranger?" Emmet asked.

Joann cupped his face and looked into his watery eyes. "She kept him because she loved him. There's nothing like knowing a life grows inside you. And, Emmet, you were *not* a stranger. She wanted me to tell you... you were the first man she ever loved. She thought she loved her ex-boyfriend, but she said, you made her feel treasured, loved, and wanted. Something she never felt before. She loved you, Emmet. Granted, it was only a short two-week thing, but I want to thank you. You gave my little girl something she always wanted. You gave her the chance to know true love and you gave her her son."

"I just wish…"

"What?"

"I wish I could thank her," he admitted. "Trevor means everything to me, the greatest gift anyone ever gave me, and I can't even thank her for it."

"Yes, you can."

"How?"

"By loving and raising your son."

Emmet took a deep breath and slowly nodded. "I did care for her, Joann, deeply. I don't believe in love anymore, but what I felt for her was as close to it as I can admit."

"I understand, honey. Don't cut yourself off from love. It's a wonderful thing and it hurts like hell when something goes wrong, and you feel like you have to be strong for everyone. Well, Emmet O'Quinn you do not have to be strong with me. I know I'm not your mother, but I know a little about what you're going through."

A weight lifted from his shoulders and he took a breath, the first truly deep and satisfying breath he had taken since Mara left him. "Thank you," he said.

"You're welcome. Now, let's eat and if you'd like, we can tell you all about the mother of your son. But one thing, mister. I *never* want to hear you *ever* say you don't deserve our friendship and love. You gave our daughter something to live for and you made her last few years happy."

The side of Emmet's mouth ticked up. "I'll always regret not going after her."

"The mother in me wants to say *good*, but you can't live

in regret."

"And I'm sorry I asked why she kept the baby. I didn't mean…"

"Oh, honey, I know. It's okay. Now, come on, let's eat. I think I heard Trevor come down."

Emmet took the washcloth from the back of his neck and wiped it down his face. He had cried until his face felt numb. He couldn't let his son see him weak like that but as he washed his hands and walked out of the restroom following Joann, the weight that lifted earlier stayed gone. Hearing Joann confirm to him he hadn't made Jennifer's life worse simply for being an idiot and not wearing protection their last time, helped him tremendously. Hearing she loved him filled him with regret. He didn't know why he was acting an emotional mess. He never cried as hard as he cried in the bathroom, even when his mother passed away. It made him want to check to make sure he didn't lose his balls somewhere over the Atlantic. Almost as if she was in the room, he could hear his ma say he had reason to be emotional and it would help him in the long run if he let it out. He wanted to be around for his son for a long time and bottling up his angst and emotions would only lead to pain down the road. Still, Trevor needed him solid and loving, not an emotional wreck.

Walking back into the kitchen, his eyes scanned the area. Sure enough, Trevor was bouncing as he sat on the stool Emmet had given up. He turned and squealed.

"Daddy, look! Look what Uncle Derek made for me! It's green just like I-land!"

"That's amazing," Emmet smiled at his son's attempt to pronounce Ireland and dropped a kiss on his head. Peter waved and he winked at him.

"What were you doing in the bathroom?" Trevor asked.

"Washing up," Emmet showed his hands. "Did you wash your hands?"

Trevor looked proud. "I did it all by myself!"

"Good on ya, lad," Emmet grinned. "Now, let's eat. I was told your Uncle Derek is a good cook."

"The best! Besides Gramma."

Emmet chuckled. "Smart boy," he beamed at Joann.

Taking a moment to look around the room, his heart still hurt at the missing faces of his family. But as Joann's words sunk in, he smiled. This was his son's family and by default his as well. They may not be his blood, but they took him as their own and though he missed his family back home, he would make the best of it, just as his father said.

America was his new home. The land of the free and home of the brave. The land across the sea.

an deireadh

Acknowledgements

Thank you so much for reading! When I was writing Emmet's story, *Across the Irish Sea* the words *four years later* hit my editor hard! Since then, I have heard from several of my fans saying how they were not ready for that! I knew then, I wanted to write something for him. And I also didn't want to give Emmet up just yet! I hope you enjoyed this short story!

Never fear! Trevor and Peter are revisited. Trevor has his own story now available! *In Dublin Fair City* takes place twenty years after the event in this book. Peter also makes an appearance but his story is revealed further in *The Song of Heart's Desire.*

Please read on for a sneak peek at *In Dublin Fair City,* book one in *Love Among the Shamrocks Collection: The Next Generation!*

love among the shamrocks collection
the next generation
Book One

In Dublin Fair City

M. KATHERINE CLARK

Prologue

Trinity College Dublin

He looked around the opulent theater lobby seeing other guests in tuxes, ball gowns, and masks of varying styles. There were delicate masks, traditional black silk masks, doctor's masks from the time of the plague with their long noses and intricate designs, comedy-tragedy masks, colorful masks, masks that covered the entire face, the top half, or the side, animal masks, character masks, scary masks, elegant masks, anything one could think of, danced, mingled, and drank all around him.

He glanced down at his modern tuxedo. The jacket was fitted, a mark from his grandfather always telling him, a well-fitted suit told a lot about a man, and a white button up shirt, lined with a strip of black silk, and black round buttons. He had debated for nearly twenty minutes if he wanted to wear a tie, bowtie, or leave the top two buttons undone. Eventually, time was the determining factor and as he slipped on his black, red, and gold Venetian mask, he had tossed the strip of black that hung around his neck onto his bed and left his flat.

Standing in the Trinity College theater holding a glass of

whiskey, hearing the music, and seeing the dancers pair off, he dampened his nerves. The fifteen-foot Christmas tree stood off to the side near the bar decorated in gold, red, and green and of course their school colors of cool blue and steel grey lined the bar. The ivory walls were covered in ornate gold ormolus of vines, leaves, and pillar crowns. Beautiful statues of Greek gods looked down on him and he remembered how he felt the first time he stepped into the theater. It was breathtaking.

After a moment of admiration, he felt the hair on the back of his neck stand on end. Turning to the grand stair, he saw her. She stood at the top of the staircase, her off the shoulder sweetheart neckline red dress popped against the ivory-gold of the wall behind her. Her delicate Venetian swan mask gracefully covered the top part of her face, coming down to the middle of her nose, the left side fanned up like a swan's wing. She looked stunning, just the way he knew she would. Their eyes locked and he saw the flicker of surprise then the heat of a blush flushed her cheeks. But he caught no hint of recognition.

Good, all is going according to plan, he thought.

She started down the stairs, her eyes never leaving his. The side of his mouth ticked up as he saw the quick rise and fall of her chest and the flush coloring her neck. She stood two steps above him, but they were eye to eye, and she had yet to drop his gaze. It was now or never. Taking a deep breath, he channeled his father's deeper and heavily Irish accented voice to disguise his own.

"I've been waiting for you," he stated.

"Me?" she questioned.

"Aye," he replied, happy with his impersonation.

"Why? Do I know you?"

"Wouldn't you know me, if you did?"

"There's a lot of students here," she answered, and he smiled at her slight American accent. "Your mask is brilliant and covering most of your face. If I'm supposed to, I'm sorry," she shook her head, then her eyes narrowed. "There is something"

"Something?"

"Familiar… I feel like I do know you. What's your name? Take off the mask?" She reached up to remove it, but he gently caught her wrist stopping her.

He shook his head. "No, Cassie," he said. "You don't need to know me, yet."

"Please?"

"Dance with me," he offered.

She stared at him again for a long moment. "Why do I get the feeling my life will change depending on the answer?"

He said nothing, just placed his empty glass on the tray of a passing waiter and offered his hand to her. Cassie looked at the hand, then him.

"Please, tell me your name."

He thought a moment and when he heard the orchestral start playing *Music of the Night* from the *Phantom of the Opera*, he nodded.

"You can call me Phantom."

"Phantom?" she questioned with a grin. "That's not a name."

"It's enough of one," he replied. "Trust me."

"Trust is easy to come by, but a second chance rarely

happens."

He said nothing for a long moment waiting for her to slip her hand into his. She didn't hesitate. Walking over to the dancefloor, he took her hand and placed his other on the small of her back. In that moment, he was eternally grateful to his stepmother for teaching him how to dance.

The tempo was slow, and they danced together not speaking but never dropping each other's gazes.

"I've always cared for you, Cassie. I need you to know that. I suppose I am concerned about your reaction so that is why I do not tell you who I am. I don't mean to scare you or anything like that, but I have to tell you... I love you. I have for a couple years now. And aye, I'm not some stalker. You do know me. I even can claim the distinction of being a friend."

"I have several friends."

"I know," he answered. "That is why I am not being any more specific. Just know, if you need me, I'll always be there for you."

"How will I know how I feel if you don't tell me who you are? I could very easily be in love with you."

"Give me a task. Anything. I will do what you ask and come to you without the mask, only me and you can decide then if you want me or not."

Cassie stared into his eyes and just as the music climaxed, she nodded.

"Okay, Phantom," she smiled. "I have something I want you to get for me."

"Name it and it's yours."

Chapter One

Five Months Later

Trevor O'Quinn looked up and across the lawn toward the entrance to the Old Library of Trinity College in Dublin to see his half-brother and sister rushing over to him. There on a visit to see if it was where they wanted to go to school, Killian and Aoife laughed together before breathlessly coming to a stop in front of him.

Trevor smiled and closed the music book he was studying, stood from the park bench, and hugged his younger siblings.

"Well?" He asked. "How was it?"

"The tour was okay," Killian started, "But since I had already seen everything with da', it was somewhat boring."

"Same," Aoife replied. "But Uni guys are hot."

"Aoife," Trevor warned. "You're sixteen. You don't know what hot means... right?"

She just giggled at his overprotective brotherliness and continued. "I wish you could have joined us."

"I know, guys, I'm sorry. I had class," he explained. "But, hey, let's go across the way and get some coffee."

Aoife made a cute disgusted sound. "You know I don't drink that stuff. Icky black ink."

"Blame the American in me," Trevor winked. "I can't get enough of the stuff."

"Da' says we'll have to learn to love it when we go to University," Killian answered as they walked toward the archway exit to the little coffee shop near campus.

"Da' is right," Trevor replied. "When you spend all night studying and have an eight am class, trust me, coffee is a lifesaver."

Waiting until it was safe to cross the street, Trevor took a moment to watch his twin brother and sister and smiled. It had been seventeen years since he and his father Emmet and stepmom Mara had left America to go back to Ireland and though those first two years Trevor barely understood what was going on at his *Gaelscoil,* he was happy to be in his father's homeland. But soon, with his Uncle Sean's tutelage, he was able to excel and was accepted to one of the finest schools in the world, his father's *Alma Mater,* Trinity College in Dublin.

Since they moved back, his cousins both older and younger had been his best friends, at least until his twin younger brother and sister were born. Then he had the siblings he always wanted. They had been close ever since.

"Trev?" Aoife's voice cleared his mind and he focused on

his siblings standing on the other side of the road. He gave an awkward laugh and wave then hurriedly crossed the street.

"Sorry," he said. "My mind drifted."

"Everything okay?" Killian asked.

"Yeah sorry, honestly I was thinking about my first few years here in Ireland. It's nothing."

"We're definitely glad you, Mum, and Da' came back. I can't imagine growing up anywhere else," Aoife said.

"American isn't bad," Trevor replied.

"No, just, there's nothing like Ireland," she clarified.

"I'm right there with you," Trevor agreed.

They pushed the door open and stepped into the coffee shop. The smell of freshly ground coffee and chocolate assaulted their noses. Trevor took a deep breath and smiled, letting out a satisfied sound.

"My grampa always says there's nothing like the smell of fresh grounds," he said.

"No, thank you," Aoife teased. "I'll take a hot chocolate."

"One hot chocolate and a spiced orange cake, got it," he winked. "Can you get us a table?"

She nodded and with a thank you, she headed to a four topper by the window. Trevor and Killian stood together in line at the café.

"So, what do you think?" Trevor asked.

"What about?" Killian replied.

"About college? Have you told Mum and Dad what you told

me?"

Killian's eyes grew large as he glanced around to make sure no one heard him.

"Please," he started. "I told you that in confidence."

"I'm not going to say anything, but don't you think you need to tell them soon? You only have two more years until college. They should know before then."

Killian huffed a sigh and ran his hand through his dark brown hair, his ice blue eyes begged him.

"I don't know what to do," he admitted. "I feel like such a failure. Da' has so many plans. He wants me to do so much and I…"

"Hey," Trevor turned to face his brother. "Don't go there. You are your own person and our parents love you. They'll be okay."

"They'll not be very happy with my choice," he shrugged.

"Trust me, I know what that's like," Trevor clapped his brother on the shoulder. "I'll be with you, if you want. When you tell them."

His young face lit with hope. "Will you?"

"Of course! I'd be happy to," Trevor grinned. "I know how it can be to tell our parents something you think will change how they look at you but trust me, it won't. They love you."

"You know?"

"You remember the year I took off between final year and college? When I travelled with my grandparents?" At Killian's nod, he continued. "I was worried because da' did that too when he was my age and always regretted it. Said no matter how amazing his travels were, it threw the timing off. But when I told him, he was fine. Said it was my choice, my life to choose what I should do. He supported me."

"But you *went* to college... it's not the same," Killian grumbled.

"'Tis," Trevor stressed. "Anyway, enough about that. What do you want?" He indicated the menu hanging overhead. They were next in line and Killian studied the board. Once he told him and Trevor ordered, they waited for the drinks and took the number for the food. Meeting their sister at the table, she put her phone down and took her hot chocolate.

"Cheers, Trev," she leaned back in the wooden chair and took a sip.

"Careful, it'll be hot," Trevor cautioned.

"Scalding," she giggled and set it down, dabbing her eyes as tears formed.

"You all right?" he asked.

"Fine," she promised. "Just an idiot."

"We knew that," her twin winked.

"Lay off," Aoife laughed and took a glass of the ice water Trevor had ordered. "So, what were you guys talking about? It looked important."

Trevor didn't react but Killian's eyes grew wide and he looked at both of his siblings.

"Uh oh," Aoife leaned forward. "This looks fun. What happened?"

Aoife's large blue eyes danced; a finer point of her facial expressions learned directly from her mother; Mara. But the ice blue eyes were distinctly from their father, Emmet.

Trevor sighed and leaned back in his chair with his coffee. "If you really must know—"

"Oh, I must," she answered.

"I told Killian a secret," Trevor started.

"I like secrets," Aoife said.

"What I'm planning for my recital," he lied.

"Oh," she looked dejected. "That's it?"

"What do you mean, *that's it?*" Trevor chuckled. "It's a big deal."

"I was hoping for something a little more... juicy," she said.

"Juicy?" Trevor laughed. "So sorry to disappoint."

Aoife sighed and leaned back. "So, what are you planning? Final year recital is pretty big right?"

"'Tis," he answered as they accepted the two slices of cake he ordered from the barista. "Some talent scouts for master degree program usually come and it's my grade for several classes."

"How?" She asked digging into her favorite orange spiced cake.

"Not only singing but stage presence, aural skills, theory, and piano performance. They want to see it all. It's nerve-wracking. They throw shite at you just to see how you respond. One of my best friends last year was set to be best in his class and when they threw a choir back up and gave him a Mozart piece to sight read..." Trevor shook his head. "He ended up being about twentieth in his class. He warned me to be at the top of everything and be prepared for the most unexpected thing."

"Like a choir backup on a Mozart piece," Killian said. "From my limited knowledge, it's unusual. Normally Mozart is either choir or solo hardly any sort of mixing."

"You're right. Not unheard of obviously but not usual."

"So, what's this surprise you're cooking up?" his sister asked.

"I'm going to anticipate them and do something no one else has done."

"What's that?"

"You'll have to wait and see," he winked.

"No fair! You told our brother! What, is he your favorite?"

"I don't have favorites," he teased.

"So…"

Trevor looked at Killian. "Should I tell her?"

Killian shook his head, a devilish smirk on his lips. Trevor looked back at their sister and shrugged. Aoife kicked them under the table.

"Ow," Trevor bent down to rub his shin. "Damn, Aoife."

"That's what you get for not telling me," she pouted. After a second of both brothers laughing at her antics, she continued. "It's next weekend, right?"

"Saturday," Trevor nodded. "I'm ready just to get it over with."

"I bet," she said. "I don't think I could ever be a singer. The things you and Mum have to do? Getting out on stage in front of people?" she shuddered. "Scary."

"It can be," he shrugged. "But when it's something you love to do; it just makes it easy."

"Trevor?" a woman's voice called from behind him. He tried to prevent the instant smile that lifted his lips when he recognized the voice. Turning, he stood.

"Hey, Cassie," he greeted.

"Hey! How have you been? I swear I haven't seen you at all since we started this final session." she hugged him. He took a second to take a deep inhale of her perfume. She always smelled amazing. And that perfume meant something more to him. He remembered the one time he had searched high and low for it only to realize his main competition for Cassie's affections, Robbie McConaghy, heir apparent to his daddy's whiskey empire, had bought it for her and gave it to her first, successfully cutting him off.

Before he could reply, the said bastard, Robbie himself showed up and laid claim to her by an arm wrapped around her shoulders.

"There you are, baby," he said. Trevor caught her grimace.

"Yeah, hey," she answered. "I saw Trevor and wanted to say hello."

"Leave the Yank alone, you promised me lunch before our next class and I'm looking forward to dessert," he licked the shell of her ear, his eyes on Trevor.

The message was clear, *back off.*

Cassie forced a smile. "I'll see you later, Trev?" she asked.

"Yeah sure," he answered. Robbie gave him his trademarked smarmy smile saying *not going to happen.* Trevor watched them go.

Having meet Cassie his first year at Trinity, they latched on to each other when they learned their mothers were American and Trevor had yet to fully adopt an Irish accent from having lived the first few years of his life in America. Cassie's accent was subtle since she was born in Ireland but had an American accent at home while she was growing up. Sometimes she used Americanisms only Trevor and the other small handful of undergraduates from America understood. Their friendship grew over the last three years until Robbie wheedled his way in between them.

Watching them leave the café, Trevor huffed a sigh and turned back to his siblings.

"What was that?" Aoife asked.

"Hmm? Oh, um, a friend. Cassie," he sat down.

"Not her, the wanker," Aoife said.

"Aoife," Trevor scolded. "Mum will blame me if she hears you speaking like that."

"Tosh, ma knows it's da' not you. Besides, if ever there was an appropriate use for that term, it would be him."

"I agree, Trev," Killian said. "He basically licked her, claiming she was his."

"Well, they've been dating since Christmas so I would assume she is his," Trevor replied taking a drink of his coffee.

"A woman doesn't belong to a man," Aoife stated.

"That's not what I mean, Aoife and I agree with you," he said.

Aoife paused, looking over her now cooled hot chocolate, observing her brother.

"You like her," she deduced.

Trevor paused. It was on the tip of his tongue to deny it but he swore he would always be truthful with them so they would always feel comfortable coming to him with anything. Taking a deep breath, he let it out slowly.

"Aye, Aoife, I like her a lot."

"Then why do you allow him to treat her that way?"

"It's not my choice, nor is it my job to protect her. She's dating him. She chose him. There's nothing I can do."

"Bollocks," Killian replied. "You always taught me to fight for what I want. Hell, da' tells us all the time… literally… all… the… time how he had to fight for Mum. How would he feel if he knew his eldest son wasn't fighting for something he loves and wants?"

"I don't love her," Trevor defended.

"Maybe," Aoife said.

"Poor use of words," Killian replied at the same time. "What I mean is, you like her, and *he* clearly thinks of her as a possession."

"She likes you too," Aoife interjected.

"And she likes you too," Killian acquiesced. "You should give it a try."

"Leave it to my *younger* siblings to tell me what I should do with a woman," Trevor shook his head.

"We're not telling you anything Da' hasn't said before," Aoife laughed.

Killian's and Aoife's phones buzzed at the same time making them jump.

"Shite," Aoife cursed. "We got to go. The next tour is

starting in ten."

Trevor drained his mug and set it on the tray. "Let's go then."

"You don't have to walk us across the street, Trev. We're fine. Finish the coffee in the carafe. We'll see you at dinner. You're still able to meet us for dinner, right?"

"Absolutely, I'll meet you at the pub across from my flat. My last class ends at four-thirty. The tour should be over around that time."

"We have a Q&A from four-thirty 'til five so we might be late, but we'll see you around then!" Aoife threw the last few words over her shoulder as she and Killian rushed out of the café.

Trevor chuckled remembering when he went on his first college visit to a different college in Galway where his cousin Fiona was studying technology and computer science. The tour guides were sticklers for punctuality.

Pouring the last of the coffee in his mug, he hummed a song, one in his repertoire the judges might ask for and pulled out his theory prep book. Turning to the last page of the notes section, he added another little idea to his list for the recital. He wanted to surprise the judges. Knowing everyone else would be reactive to what they said, he wanted to be proactive. Maybe it was the American in him but whatever it was, he enjoyed toying with a few ideas on how to beat them at their own game.

Chapter Two

The next day flew by as everyone on campus was getting ready for their final exams and the music school worked on their juried finals. With everything piling up, Trevor hadn't had a chance to call his dad for a couple days. Something he did every evening and as he fell into bed after midnight, he pulled out his phone and clicked over to his dad's text chain.

For the first few years of his life, Emmet O'Quinn had been a larger than life unattainable entity but when his mother died, his father moved with him to America. To this day, Trevor could not remember his mother, but he missed her more than he thought possible. Those four years he and his father spent together in America were an elusive memory, but it built the foundation of their relationship. His dad became more than a dad, he was his best friend and confidant. They moved back to Ireland and Emmet and Trevor's stepmother Mara renewed their vows, but Emmet made sure Trevor was still his number one priority.

When Mara's band *Celtic Spirit* went on tour, it was only Emmet and Trevor again for a short time. But when he was on summer break, Emmet would pack Trevor up and they would meet Mara on the road in America, Australia, France, Germany, Italy, wherever she was touring, and those memories made him smile.

The birth of his twin siblings, Killian and Aoife had put an end to their travels for a time. When they were born Mara took a break from singing for three years, then went on a comeback tour but by then, Trevor was twelve and able to help his father be a stay-at-home dad. When Mara's album went platinum, Emmet took less and less time at the dealership he owned. Soon, he sold it to Trevor's Uncles Paddy and Tom, Keera's and Chloe's husbands.

It was Mara who inspired Trevor to pursue his own singing career and even had him in the studio with her occasionally. Mara always treated him as her own son even though Trevor's mother, Jennifer had died when he was two.

When one of Mara's songs came over his headphones, he smiled but as her hauntingly beautiful voice sang *Raglan Road*, tears gathered in his eyes.

This was the time of year he hated the most. He hadn't been back home to Kerry since the new year and he missed his family. All of them. Two dozen cousins, his aunts and uncles, his Grandma Dee, and Grandad Orin. He missed his Aunt Charlotte and Uncle Derek and his cousin Peter back in America and especially his gramma and grampa, his mother's parents.

He missed his old dog too. His dad had kept the promise me made to get him a dog and took him to the pound to pick out his new pet. The memory of the old slobbery face of his lab-terrier mix crossed his mind and as sad as it was to lose him three years ago, he was so happy to have the sweet memories. Emmet had buried him next to his old lab, Jacks in his grandparent's backyard.

His throat closed with emotion. Letting out an irritated grunt, Trevor wiped his tears away and turned back to his text chain with his father.

Trevor: Hey, dad, sorry I've been MIA for a couple days and couldn't call you back. I hope everything is okay. I know you would have left a message if it wasn't. Miss you and Mum. Miss talking to you but with final exams and jury coming up, my life has been eat, sleep and study... though seeing the time it's more eat and study, than sleep. Anyway, miss you, hope to talk to you soon. No need to call or text back, I know you're probably asleep. Love you. Night.

Almost before Trevor set his phone down to charge, his dad's face popped up on the screen along with his special ringtone. Trevor smiled and answered the video call. His father's face filled the screen, his ice blue eyes and red hair, so similar to Trevor's, he grinned.

"Hiya, dad."

"Oh, Trev, it's good to see you, son. How are you? How's things? How's school?" Emmet asked.

"Good, yeah, busy. Did I wake you?" Trevor asked trying to ignore how much he wanted one of his dad's hugs telling him everything would be all right.

"Nah, I was up. Watching a scary movie with your mum who fell asleep on me, so now I'm checking every door and window to make sure it's locked."

Trevor chuckled. "It's the Irish countryside, dad. What evil monsters could be lurking there?"

"Aye, well, you'll never guess where this movie took place."

"The Irish Countryside?" he guessed.

"Aye," Emmet chuckled then paused near the dining room window and turned his full attention on his son. "You doing all right, lad?"

Trevor nodded. "Just miss you."

"I miss you too, but I'll be seeing you on Saturday."

"Can't wait."

"How's things, though? Killian said he and Aoife had a great time visiting you and Trinity. It would be nice to have all my children go there."

Trevor debated but decided it was best. "You know, dad…" he started. "You might want to think of other options for them."

"Other options? Like what?"

"Like the possibility one or both may not want to go to college."

Emmet was quiet and Trevor kicked himself seeing understanding in his father's eyes. He should never have said anything. His brother may never forgive him.

"I wondered why he went. Your mother and I both know he doesn't want to go and hasn't told us yet. I'm glad he confided in you. I just hate the idea he won't get a degree. In today's job market an undergraduate degree is required for most good paying jobs."

"What do you mean?" Trevor questioned.

"Mara and I have known for a while Killian was looking at alternatives instead of university. We haven't said anything to him, hoping he would come to us himself, but he hasn't yet."

"Maybe mention in passing that it's all right not to go? That you wouldn't be disappointed in him," Trevor offered.

"I could never be disappointed in any of my children. Does he honestly think that?"

"I know nothing," Trevor replied. "I've already said too much."

"Of course," Emmet agreed. "I'm glad he knows he can confide in you. I'll say nothing about you mentioning it to me."

"Only because I worry about him."

"We both do, he's sixteen, you remember how it was back then."

"God, do I ever," Trevor chuckled. "It was brutal."

"It was for me too, yeah," Emmet replied. "Sixteen was… difficult."

They were silent a moment just staring at each other until Emmet cleared his throat. "So, are you ready for your jury Saturday?"

"I think so, yeah. Though as mum says you're never completely ready and that's okay."

"She definitely says that, so she does," Emmet answered. "Have you given any more thought to grad school?"

Trevor had brought it up at Christmas recess and had been met with encouragement but the more he thought about and researched it, the more school in America appealed to him. But the thought of leaving his family for a solid two years made his heart hurt. He didn't know how his dad had been able to leave Ireland for a midsized big city in the heartland of Middle America for three and a half years when Trevor was a child before Mara came back into their lives.

"I have but I'm not sure."

"Why's that?" Emmet asked.

"Well, for one it's expensive and two I don't know if I could be away from you all for that long."

"Don't worry about the money. Your mother left you that college fund and over the years I've been fortunate enough to add to it. You're set for grad school, if you want."

"It's not that, dad," he answered. "Not only."

"Being away from us?" he questioned.

Trevor nodded. "Yeah, I miss you guys so much right now and I'm only four hours away here."

"You've been away before. That time you went to stay with your Aunt Charlotte and Uncle Derek while your mum and I went on her comeback tour."

"I was twelve, it was an adventure," Trevor justified.

"Okay," Emmet chuckled. "Well, then the time you went travelling with your grandparents."

"I know but I had them with me. If I go to grad school in America, I'll be alone for two to three years."

Emmet was quiet for a long moment, but his eyes gave him away. "America?" His voice was tight.

Trevor clamped his mouth shut. He hadn't meant to let it slip.

"You're looking at grad schools in America?" Emmet clarified.

Taking a fortifying breath, Trevor plowed ahead.

"Yeah," he admitted. "I am. They're the best schools for opera besides Italy, of course. And as a citizen, it's easier to get in. I haven't done anything," he hurried. "I've only looked."

Emmet cleared his throat softly. "Well, Trev if that's your desire, I back you. I'll miss you. But I back you. I would never want to stand in the way of your dreams."

"I know that. I just don't think I could be on my own that far away… never mind, you know what? My dad never taught me to be scared. He always taught me to follow my dreams and that's what I need to do."

A wide grin spread across Emmet's face. "That's my lad," he stated. "But now, tell me, any news on the other finals? How's studying going?"

Talking to his dad until well past one in the morning, Trevor signed off with a *talk soon* and *I love you*. Placing his phone on the nightstand, he pulled off his t-shirt and sweatpants. Flopping down onto the mattress in his boxers, he turned on the television and turned off the light.

Copyright © 2020 by M. Katherine Clark

Made in the USA
Middletown, DE
12 March 2023

26618771R00033